The One Nigh

Piper S. Grey

All rights reserved. No part of this publication may be reproduced, stored, or transmitted in any form or by any means, electronic, mechanical, photocopying, recording, scanning, or otherwise without written permission from the author. It is illegal to copy this book, post it to a website, or distribute it by any means without permission.

This novel is a work of fiction. The names, characters, and incidents portrayed in it are the work of the author's imagination.

THE ONE NIGHT VALENTINE

February 14 2024

Copyright © 2024 Piper S. Grey

Written by Piper S. Grey

THE ONE NIGHT VALENTINE

TABLE OF CONTENTS

Chapter 1 ---------------------------------- 7

Chapter 2 ---------------------------------- 15

Chapter 3 ---------------------------------- 24

Chapter 4 ---------------------------------- 38

Chapter 5 ---------------------------------- 58

Epilogue ----------------------------------- 70

Coming soon -------------------------------- 73

More by the Author ------------------------- 74

About the Author --------------------------- 75

Piper S. Grey

THE ONE NIGHT VALENTINE

THE ONE NIGHT VALENTINE

Piper S. Grey

For my forever Valentine.

THE ONE NIGHT VALENTINE

Piper S. Grey

CHAPTER ONE

I watch the revolving door of the Ritz-Carlton hotel in Toronto. Sitting on the beige couch in the lobby, I look down at the watch on my wrist, checking the time. I was supposed to meet a date at the hotel - Stuart. A corporate lawyer working for RTE Corp, one of the largest fuel companies in Canada. In other words, not someone I would normally go out with. We met at a friend's birthday party the week prior. Not having gone on a date in months, I agreed.

One thing to know about me - I hate being late. A nagging voice in my brain would scream the passing minutes if I wasn't on time. Nevertheless, I sat in the hotel lobby waiting for Stuart, who was already late. To our first date. Who does that? I wasn't really attracted to him all that much. But after showing up late to our *first* date, there was not going to be a second.

A part of me wants to just get up and leave, but my conscience doesn't let me stand the guy up – that is if he ever shows.

As the minutes pass, I watched people, fancy, probably rich, people walk in and out of the Ritz-Carlton. I twiddle my thumbs in my lap, wishing I had brought a book to keep me occupied. Although, who would have ever thought I would be sitting in the lobby of one of the most prestigious hotels in Toronto, waiting for a date that was unlikely to show. Kind of embarrassing.

    The elevator doors open, and I turn my head to look at the people walking out of it. Men in handsome suits, women in beautiful dresses and high heels, and occasionally a child being guided by their parents. Amongst the handful of people leaving the elevator is a handsome man, wearing a dark blue suit. His hair neatly combed over to the right, with a single stray wisp falling onto his forehead. He adjusts his cufflinks as he walks over to the front desk, leaning onto the counter, speaking to the young woman behind the computer. I watch the young woman's face go red, as she speaks to the man across her. I've had enough crushes in my life to know that behind her straight face, she was suppressing lots of emotions. Well, sure. Who wouldn't? He is gorgeous. While the woman turns to look at the computer, the man straightens his back and looks over his shoulder. He scans the lobby, and his eyes met mine. The corner of his lip curls into a smile. My cheeks go hot, and I turn my gaze back to the revolving front door. Great timing too – Stuart walked in.

I stand up and straighten my dark green dress and walk towards Stuart. He leans in for a hug and I sneak a glance at the man near the front desk. He is clearly watching us, only this time the smile is gone. Instead, he's eyeing Stuart. Or is he eyeing me? Who could tell, really?

"I'm so sorry I'm late." Stuart snapped me back into reality, "We lost some papers at the office, delivery problems or something. Have you been here long?"

"Umm – no. Not at all." I smiled backed at him.

He placed his hand around my waist and guided me toward the hotel bar. As we walked away, I looked over my shoulder at the front desk. He was gone. The woman, however, was giggling with her colleagues. Talking about him, no doubt about it.

We sit side by side at the hotel bar counter. He had removed his suit jacket and slung it over the chairs back. His blonde hair slicked back. He kind of reminded me of Draco Malfoy, except that he is in his early thirties. The light blue button-down shirt fit snug against his skin as he reached across the counter to pick up his drink. I run my fingers up and down the cold glass, watching Stuart speak, still thinking of the handsome man from the lobby.

"I think you've heard enough about my day." Stuart chuckled, "What about you?"

I took a sip from my drink, "What about me?"

He leans back in his seat, the fabric of his shirt stretching against his chest, "What did you do at work today?"

"Nothing out of the ordinary," I put my drink back down, "My younger students wrote a test on Shakesepeare's *Othello*. I graded my older students' essays, and I had a staff meeting."

"If you're so smart, and have the opportunity to have any job you want, why do you become a teacher?" He laughs. I don't.

"I mean, your salary is close to nothing. How you can even afford to buy a dress like that, I don't know. I mean, that wasn't a smart decision, Jess."

What an ass. I signal to the bartender for a refill and pretend I didn't hear what Stuart just said. Stuart takes a swig of his drink, watching me intently. I grab my glass and bring it to my lips, avoiding Stuart's gaze. He doesn't take his eyes off me. He leans forwards and rests his elbows on his knees, his glass still in hand. He squints his eyes, and a grin appears across his face.

"Tell me, "He starts, his voice going lower, "how does a pretty little *thing* like you stay single?" He extends his right hand

and pulls a strand of my blonde hair behind my ear. My grip tightens around the glass as panic begins to set. He leans closer to my ear.

"If you were mine, Jessica, I would never let you out of my sight."

Stuart reaches to touch my cheek, but I move backwards in my chair.

"Yes, well, I'm pretty good at filtering out the creepy guys." I retort.

His smile twists into something of anger and he returns to a sitting straight. I grab my purse and stand up, "Excuse me, but I need to go use the restroom."

He grumbles something under his breath as I walk past him and out into the lobby, searching for the nearest bathroom. I fight back tears as I duck my head down and break out into a jog towards the bathroom. I make it halfway across before someone grabs me by my shoulders. It's a firm grip that stops me in my tracks. The hands wrapped around my whole upper arm, and a warm, deep voice laughed out.

"Woah, careful there."

I bring my face up to eye level and in front of me is a lot of – chest? Chest and a dark blue suit. I look up and see the chiseled face of the man from the hotel lobby earlier that evening. My mouth opens to speak but no words come out and I end up staring at this man who looks like he was built by Greek Gods.

    He laughs and rubs my arms. Damn. His dentist must love him. His teeth looked like those models you see in dental commercials. Maybe he was one of those models.

    "You know, most people won't like you running into them as much as I do. You be careful." He winked at me with his dark green eyes and continued walking through the hotel. I stand in my spot, unable to move. Did he just wink at me? No one has ever winked at me. No one that gorgeous has ever looked at me either. I brushed my long bangs out of my face and wet my lips. Too stunned to walk, I click my heels together and cross my arms. I bring my hand up to cover my mouth and smile into my palm.

    I can feel my cheeks go hot and red as I walk to the bathroom, this time my pace much slower.

    I enter the bathroom and stand in front of the mirror. I stared into the mirror, watching the blonde-haired young woman stare back at me. I placed both my hands on the counter and leaned my weight on them, tucking my head down towards my chest and closing my eyes. I stay there for what feels like hours but could not have been more than just a few seconds. I lift my head back up and begin fixing my hair.

Piper S. Grey

Just a bit longer. Keep it together, Jess. A bit longer and then you never need to speak to that asshole ever again.

Out of the corner of my eye I notice a woman in a badass pantsuit smiling at me. We make eye contact, and she makes her way over to me.

"Bad date?" She asks, her short hair bouncing as she walks.

"Oh yeah..." I say, still playing with my hair.

The woman stops to my right and leans her back against the counter, crossing her arms in front of herself. "Bit of a dick?" she raises an eyebrow.

I smile at her, noticing the deep blue colour of her eyes. "Sounds like you've met him."

She shakes her head smiling "I've had a lot of business meetings here, and I've witnessed a LOT of women on sucky dates." She cocks her head to the side, the bangs of her pixie cut hair dropping to the side, "May I suggest – if he's not your boyfriend, maybe end things tonight so you don't need to break up with him on Valentine's Day tomorrow. Breaking up with someone on February 13th is still better than breaking up with someone on February 14th."

I nod a small thanks and drop my eyes to the sink.

She stands up, walking towards the bathroom exit. She stops just before the door and turns back to face me before saying, "Hey, you deserve better than that asshole."

She smiles at me and exits the bathroom. I never saw her after that, but her words stayed with me for a very long time.

CHAPTER TWO

I sit at the bar with Stuart. The buzz from the alcohol drowning out his voice that seemed to get more annoying with every passing minute. I watch the liquid in my glass swirl as Stuart went on with his millionth story about RTE Corp.

RTE – ruin the environment?

I lazily lift my gaze and noticed the brown-haired man I ran into sitting behind a table with a group of men in equally expensive suits. Why couldn't I have been on a date with him? Why did it have to be Stuart?

I watch him bring his glass to his lips and take a small sip before smiling at the men around the table. His teeth were incredibly straight and white. I focus in on his smile, wondering how much he's spent on dental work. Did he ever drink coffee or pop? Surely not if his teeth are that white and unstained. I suddenly become very aware of my own teeth. I quickly brushed my tongue against the tips of my top teeth, wondering just how stained my teeth looked. I took another sip of my drink, still looking straight past Stuart towards the extremely hot, mystery man. He was now speaking to his group, his right hand resting on the table. His button-down shirt sleeve starting at his wrist, my gaze following from the tips of his fingers, up the sleeve to his torso. The button-down shirt lying flat against his chest, defined muscles visible through the fabric. Taking another sip of my drink, my mind begins to wander, fantasizing what he must look like under that suit. Slowly removing each layer so I could take all of him in, running my hands down his body.

He turns his head, and our eyes meet. He presses his lips together and his eyes darken. My cheeks go hot, and I take another sip. I can feel his eyes on me. He doesn't stop staring. I swallow hard watching him. Jeez – how long can he stare at someone. Okay, this is getting uncomfortable. I turn my attention back to Stuart.

"... So, we didn't want him to think the operation was a failure." He was reciting a story. Something about work probably. Does he ever shut up? Does he have a life outside work?

I nod, trying to make it look like I have been listening. He's so self-absorbed though I doubt he even noticed that I spaced out while he was speaking.

I'm looking at Stuart, but my mind is circling in thoughts of the tall, handsome man. Was he single? Of course, he wasn't. Who wouldn't want to be with him? Either way, he wouldn't be interested in me. His girlfriend was probably a Victoria's Secret model. Super tall. Skinny. Nice legs. Warm tan. Probably has done work for Habitat for Humanity. Super rich. In other words, she was probably everything I wasn't.

My head began to spin. Some lucky girl out there got to come home to a boyfriend like hot mystery man, while I was here on a date with Stuart, drowning myself in drinks to not have to listen to his dull voice, and never-ending work stories. I watch hot mystery man across the bar, sitting behind the table, chatting to the group he was with. Having no knowledge of my existence.

I'm lost in my thoughts and I guess Stuart picked up on that. He grabs me by my wrist and holds a strong grip. I spin my head to face Stuart and try to pull my hand away from him.

"What are you doing?" my voice shakes.

"Yo-you have b-been ignoring me all evening." His words slur, and I can tell he's had a bit too much to drink.

"Stuart. Let go of me." I try to keep my voice as straight and stern as possible. I'm not going to give in to some drunk man.

"Come on honey – let's go get a hotel r-room. I can show you a goo-good time, baby." His fingers tighten around my wrist as I try to wriggle out of his grip.

"Stuart, you're scaring me. Let. Go." My voice raises.

THE ONE NIGHT VALENTINE

"You. You owe me, Jessica. I tried *hiccup* to show you a nice evening, b-but you. You. You ignored me. So now. You. Owe. Me. Imma go and fuck you now. *Hiccup.*"

I can smell the alcohol off his breath as he moves his face closer to mine. I try to pull my wrist free from his grip, but the more I writhe under his touch, the more he tightens his fingers.

"No. Stuart, you're hurting me." My voice breaks.

"Hey." A deep, familiar voice barked. Stuart and I both look up.

It was him. Hot mystery man. He towered overtop of us. There was a dark look in his eyes as he glared at Stuart. He took a step closer to us, and calmly spoke again. "The lady said 'No'. Let go of her." It was scary how calmly he spoke. He articulated every letter. Stuart stood up to face the man, letting go of my wrist with one swift throw.

"Who the hell are you, telling me what to do?" Stuart spits. The man stands still.

"I am just a man standing up to a jerk." He stands looking down at Stuart. Never blinking.

"Now, the lady told you 'No', so I suggest you leave."

"Oh y-yeah? *Hiccup.* What will you do if I d-don't?"

Hot mystery man chuckles, "You see that man by the exit?" He pointed towards a tall man standing by the exit of the bar. He's dressed in all black and has an earpiece. He has his arms crossed in front of him and keeps his eyes glued to Stuart. He looks as though he were a bodyguard or something.

Woah. How rich was this guy? The longer I looked at his bodyguard the more convinced I become that he probably has killed someone. I wouldn't be surprised if it was with his bare hands.

"That is Michael. You don't want to meet him. But, if you continue to disrespect your date, you will meet him." Continued the man. As if on cue, Michael balls his hand into a fist, and I swear I hear some bones crack.

Stuart glances over at Michael and back at the tall man. He scowls and begins to make his way out the bar.

I unconsciously rub my wrist and bring my hands against my chest. Hot mystery man keeps his eyes on Stuart until he is out of sight.

Once Stuart was gone, he sits down on the stool beside me and rests his elbows on his knees, leaning over towards me. A soft smile crossing his face.

"You alright?" He gestures toward my wrist.

"Umm yeah. I umm – thanks." I blush. My head is pounding. The alcohol now clearly getting to my brain. I rub at my eyes with my thumb and index finger.

He stares at me a little while longer and turns to the bartender.

"Could you put her drinks on my tab, please." The bartender nods and hot mystery man turns back to face me.

"That was probably the worst date I've ever been on." I chuckle, looking down into my lap. He continues to stare at me. His smile soft and warm. His lips - inviting.

"Are you staying at the hotel?" He asks, his voice deep, and smooth.

"No, I live not too far away." I shake my head, "I actually should probably go find a taxi or something."

"Don't worry about that. I have a driver on standby in front of the hotel. He can drive you home." He tilts his head ever so slightly as he speaks. His eyes darting down to find my lips.

"Oh, I really shouldn't. I don't want to be an inconvenience."

"It's not an inconvenience. I'm staying at the hotel this weekend for some business. I won't need my car, or my driver, tonight. I would much rather you get home safely."

I open my mouth to oppose but I'm not feeling well, and it would be nicer than having to hunt down a taxi this late on a Friday night. So instead, I smile shyly, and give him a small nod.

His eyes darken as he keeps eye contact with me. I inhale sharply through my teeth and lower my gaze. He stands from his stool and extends a hand out toward me. My eyes jump from his hand to his face. Hesitantly I rest my fingers onto his palm, and he gently closes his big hand around my fingers. His hands are warm. Soft, and strong. I rise out of my seat, adjusting the bottom of my dress with my free hand. I notice his eyes dart from my face to the hem of my dress and back up. I stand for a moment, getting used to my buzzed centre of gravity. He stands patiently waiting for me. I look up into his eyes and feel a warm sensation in the bottom of my stomach. I turn back to my stool grabbing my coat and throwing it on. It's thin and worn, and nowhere near good enough for the cold Canadian February temperature. But it's better than no coat at all. He offers me the crook of his elbow and I weave my arm through and rest my hand on his forearm. With a shadow of a smile, he turns his head and begins towards the exit of the bar. I follow.

As we exit outside the hotel, a black Cadillac Escalade stands in the porte cochere. As we approach the car, a tall man climbs out and walks over to the back door and opens it. I immediately recognized him as Michael.

Is he not a bodyguard like I thought? Is he actually a driver?

Hot mystery man moves his arm to place his hand on the small of my back, guiding me into the back seat. Once I climb into the car, Michael closes the door gently. The mystery man says something to him and Michael nods. I can't hear what he said and in no way was I able to read his lips. So, I relax against the back of the seat. It was warm inside the car. It wasn't a far walk to the car, but even just a few seconds outside in Canada mid-February, you could feel the cold.

I watch hot mystery man walked around the back of the car. Michael following him. He climbs into the backseat next to me as Michael gets in the driver's seat. I lean closer to Michael and recite my address. He types it into the screen on the dashboard. I lean back into my seat and exhale as the car slides into motion.

He sits at the opposite end of the backseat, his dark eyes still watching me.

"Do you mind me asking?" He starts, his voice smooth as butter, "Why were you on a date with that jerk anyway?"

I turn my head to look at him and begin twiddling my thumbs. His voice deep and sexy, I could listen to it all night.

"I met him at my friend's party. He seemed alright. Plus, it's not everyday someone wants to go out with a teacher."

"You're a teacher?"

"Umm, yeah. High school English."

His chest expands as he takes a deep breath in. His eyes fixated on mine. I swallow hard, trying to ignore the feeling that was growing between my legs. I look out the window and close my eyes.

I imagine him walking up to me, shirtless, his navy-blue suit pants low. As he approaches me, he growled my name. He needs me. He stops himself mere centimeters away from me. I can smell his cologne wafting off his body. He stares deep into my eyes, a ferocious animal-like hunger in his. He cups my face with his massive hands and parts my lips with his. He kisses me with intent. He needs this just as much as I do. He moves away from me and drops his hands. His lips linger over top mine as his hands reach down and graze my hipbones. I let out a small whimper into his mouth. My eyes close, and I rest my forehead on his. His hand moves from my hipbone, down my thigh, and his long fingers slide up my legs. He put his lips against my ear, and in his deep voice said, "Hey, we're here."

CHAPTER THREE

My eyes shoot open. I can feel my heart still racing. How long was I asleep for? I look around and notice my apartment building outside the car. We are home. Draping over my shoulders and torso was a navy-blue suit coat. It was his. I look over at him, immediately remembering the dream I just had.

"You fell asleep." He smiles gently, "But we're here."

"Oh. Thank you." I prop myself up off the car door.

"Let me help you out." He says as he climbs out of the car and walks around to get my door. I look over at Michael and say softly "Thank you for the ride. I really appreciate it."

He looks at me through the rear-view mirror and nods gently. I'm fairly certain I saw him smile. I didn't know he did that. My car door opens, and hot mystery man helps me out. His coat still around my shoulders. I begin removing it, but he puts a strong hand on my shoulder, stopping me.

"I have plenty at home. Keep it. As a memento of our time together." The corner of his mouth breaking into a smile. He places his hand on my lower back, and we walk into the building together.

He walks me all the way up to my apartment. The whole time we walked in silence. As we approach my door, I turn to face him.

"Well, this is it." I point to the door. He's towering overtop me, softly smiling. His hands are in his pockets.

"Thank you again, for helping me out back at the bar. I'm not sure how I can repay you." I speak softly. I don't want my roommate to overhear.

He looks down at his shoes and lifts his eyes at me.

"I'll tell you what." He takes half a step toward me. He puts a hand inside his shirt pocket and brings out a small business card. With his other hand he brings a pen out of his pants pocket and scribbles something on the card. He extends it out to me. "I'm in town for business for the weekend. Promise to call me when you need me." He raises his eyebrows.

I take the business card from him and admire it. The design is sleek, with various shades of grey.

Maverick Walker
Walker Publications
Maverick@WalkerPublications.com

Underneath, the phone number was crossed out and a new one scribbled on. So, his name is Maverick. *Houston, we have a name!* I shoot my eyes up at Maverick.

"Jessica." He raises an eyebrow at my outburst.

"My name is Jessica. I realize I never introduced myself."

"I think it's wonderful. Really suits you." He chuckles.

My cheeks go red, and I reach into my coat pocket to get my keys.

"Good night. Jessica." He smiles at me and starts his way down the hall to the elevator. He doesn't look back. I watch him walk down the hall, taking in all of him. I'm never going to see him again. I close my eyes, my headache now pounding against my skull. I wiggle the key into the lock and open the door.

I walk into kitchen the following morning. My roommate, Catherine, is already sitting at the kitchen table, drinking a cup of coffee, scrolling through her phone.

"Well look at you!" She says, a bit too loud for my hungover brain. I walk over to the coffee machine and begin to scoop some ground coffee.

"You didn't get home until late last night. I stayed up as long as I could but ended up going to bed." She rests her chin in the palm of her hand and watches me from across the kitchen. I briefly glance at her and go back to the coffee machine.

"So, how was he?" She asks in a sing-song voice.

I place my mug on the counter with a small thump and glare at Catherine. I turn my body to face her and cross my arms.

"You mean Stuart? He was a jerk." I bark at her. Catherine's smile disappears and she sits staring at me. Her eyebrows furrowing.

"First off, he came incredibly late. Second, he was so rude. Third, he got drunk and tried to force me into bed with him."

"Oh no, Jess, I'm so sorry."

"Yeah well, that's the last time I'm seeing him."

"I didn't know he would be such a jerk. He didn't seem that bad before. You know, I just thought – "

"It's fine. It's over." I turn back to the coffee machine and begin pouring coffee into my light pink 'Yes, I really do need all these books' mug. I can feel Catherine's eyes on me. I turn around, mug in hand, and lean back against the counter, bringing the mug to my lips. Catherine, still watching me, smirks. She has one of her evil Catherine grins. The one where you know she figured something out and was now going to use it against you.

"What?" I ask, my eyes widening.

"You met someone." She bites her thumb.

Evil, I tell you. How could she possibly know? Surely, I don't have 'I met the handsomest guy ever last night, he saved me from a drunk, drove me home, gave me his phone number, and now I can't stop thinking about him, and may be developing some sort of unhealthy obsession with him.' Written across my forehead.

"What makes you think I met someone?" I ask quizzically.

Catherine leans forwards, scrunching her eyes.

"Because I know you, Jess. We've been friends since the beginning of university."

I roll my eyes and take another sip of my coffee. I swear my headache eases with every hot sip.

"Oh, come on! I *know* you met someone! Tell me about him! Or is it a girl?"

"Alright, fine. His name is Maverick. Maverick Walker."

Catherine chokes on her coffee.

"Maverick Walker?"

I make my way over to the kitchen table and sit down next to her.

"Do you know him?"

"Are you kidding? He's a titan in the publishing industry! He seeks out small indie authors through social media and then publishes their books. He has a way of finding the hidden gems of books. Basically, every author that goes through his company becomes a best seller. Oh, what I wouldn't give to work for him."

I run my fingers up and down the side of my mug, taking in every word Catherine was saying.

She bites down on her thumb lost in thought before shooting her eyes up at me and asking, "Do you think you could introduce me?"

"What? Cat, I barely even know him. He just helped me get Stuart off me."

She stares at me waiting for more.

"And he drove me home."

Catherine didn't move. Her smile wide like the Cheshire Cat.

"Well, his driver drove me. We sat in the backseat."

Jeez, she can pull anything out of me. Why am I even friends with her?

"And then he walked me up to the apartment."

I'm certain her smile grew even wider. Like that was possible.

"That's it! Then I went home, and he went back to the hotel."

"Ugh, Jess. I'm so happy for you. Tell me, is he as gorgeous in person as he is in photos?"

I lean back in my chair and look down at my mug. I blush and fight back a smile.

"Oh my god, he is!" Catherine closes her hands onto her mouth. "Tell me you gave him your number."

"He gave me his business card. And he wrote his personal number on it."

Catherine looks as though she may pass out.

"He told me that he's in town for the weekend, and that if I need anything, I should call."

Catherine begins pacing around the kitchen, barely able to contain her excitement. As she approaches the refrigerator, she suddenly stops, and whips her head around.

"You need to call him."

"No."

Catherine stomps her way over to me, grabs the mug out of my hands, and sets it down far enough that I can't reach it.

"Jessica." She rarely calls me Jessica. "You need to call this man. He is clearly into you, and he won't be in town for long. If you don't call him, you're going to lose your chance, and then you're going to be walking around, sulking for who knows how long, and I don't want to put up with that again. Plus, if you go out with Maverick, you can tell him about me and what a wonderful editor I am and how I can be a great part of his team. Call. Him."

There's no way I'm going to call him. I am not that upfront. I have trouble telling the waiter at a restaurant that they gave me the wrong meal, how am I supposed to call a guy that I think is smoking hot and ask him out? But, to get Catherine off my back, I tell her "I'll think about it. But that's all I can promise you."

She squeals and returns to her chair and cup of coffee. She grabs her phone off the wooden kitchen table and continues her scrolling. All the while smiling, like a child in a toy store.

I reach across the table, grab my mug and get lost in my thoughts of Maverick.

I sit on the light blue couch in our small living room with my nose in my book as Catherine runs around the apartment getting ready for her date. She's putting in earrings as she walks up to me.

"Call. Him."

"Cat, you know I'm not going to do it."

She pinches the bridge of her nose and exhales. Loud.

"Jess. It is Saturday night. It is Valentine's Day. I will be home late, and when I get back you better either be gone with Maverick, or here with Maverick. Whatever you choose, Maverick must be with you."

"Even if I do call him, it's not certain that he will even want to see me."

"I mean this in the nicest way possible. You may be smart. But sometimes, you are so dumb. If he wasn't interested in you, he would not have given you his phone number. Guys don't work like that."

I stare at Catherine. Was she right?

"He also would not have driven you home. Or walked you to the door."

What she was saying didn't sound entirely wrong.

Catherine hurries to the front door, grabbing her black boots out of the closet and yanking them on.

"Now. I will have my phone on me and if you call, I will make an exception and answer. But. If you call me and you don't tell me that you are with Maverick, or waiting for Maverick, I will be so disappointed and that may just ruin the entire foundation of our relationship."

"I thought the foundation of our relationship was that we both majored in English, and both hated Professor Harte."

"Yes. Well... that too." She smiles at me. One of her signature Catherine smiles that could make you forgive any crime she may have committed. I'm fairly certain it's only a matter of time before she commits some sort of crime.

"Love you, Jess. See you whenever." She waves at me and is out the door before I have a chance to respond. I laugh shaking my head. I probably wouldn't be where I am today without Catherine. She is my rock, and now I cannot imagine my life without her.

Was she right though? Was Maverick interested? It makes sense that he wouldn't have done all that if he wasn't interested. But on the other hand, why would a handsome, successful man like him want to do with me? But what did I have to offer? I'm a 25-year-old English teacher, living with her best friend. I read books in my spare time, and I go to bed at a reasonable hour. I bore myself just thinking about it.

I close my book and look over at my phone. I tap my index finger against the cover of the book, contemplating calling Maverick. Besides, what's the worst that can happen? I profess my love to him, ask him out on a date knowing that he is well out of my league, he tells me that there was a misunderstanding and that he wasn't *actually* interested, I embarrass myself in front of the most attractive guy I have ever met, lose any chance of being in a relationship with him, and probably any other person after this much embarrassment. Okay, so what did we learn? I shouldn't call him.

I place the book down on the coffee table and head over to the kitchen to grab a drink. Catherine had opened a bottle of wine the other day and hadn't finished it, so looks like I'm going to.

I pour myself a glass, still beating myself up over whether I should call Maverick.

Do you think he ever goes by Mav?

There's only one way to know. I guess I could call him.

As if on cue, I get a text from Catherine.

Catherine: CALL. HIM. NOW.

I frown. It's kind of scary how much she knows me and every single thought I have. I should probably confront her about that.

I cross my arms across my chest and head back to the living room. I fall backwards onto the couch, eyeing my phone in my hand. I take a generous swig from my wine glass and turn on the phone. I take the business card out of my pocket and read it over again.

C'mon Jess, you can do this. Just call him and tell him that you think he's hot.

I pinch the bridge of the nose. What makes me think I can just go and do this?

Stop overthinking this! Just call him. Do it quick. Like pulling a band-aid.

I exhale and open my phone, hurrying to type his number in before I regret doing this. The phone begins to ring. I stare at the screen.

Holy shit. What am I doing?

I continue staring at my phone as it rings. My heart pounds so hard against my chest that momentarily I fear my ribs may give out and shatter. My eyes widen with each ring of the phone, until *click.*

"Maverick Walker.

I hesitate and bring the phone to my ear.

"Maverick. Hi. It's Jess. From the bar. Last night. From the bar last night." I close my eyes, cringing at the words that just came out my mouth. I'm an ENGLISH teacher for god's sake.

"Jessica. I was wondering when I'd be hearing from you." His voice is smooth, and deep. He enunciates every syllable.

"How may I be of assistance to you on this fine evening?" He asks. It sounds almost as though he's smiling. Maybe he's smiling?

"Umm. Well." I exhale loudly, preparing myself for an eternity of embarrassment. "Well, you see. I have something I want to tell you. Or not so much *want,* more *need* because if I don't, I might regret it and also my roommate, Catherine, would probably kill me. She's quite scary. She wants to work at your company actually. So, I probably shouldn't have said that she's scary. She's quite lovely." Holy shit, I'm blabbering. But Maverick stays silent, listening.

"So anyways, for a multitude of reasons, including that I have been beating myself up over this all day, I have decided to call you and tell you the following: I think you are the most attractive guy I have ever met. Honestly, I don't know if you're human or if you were created by some sort of Greek god, and with the power of magic or something you found your way to Canada. If I were a Greek Goddess, I would probably stay at Mount Olympus, or at least in Greece because it's horribly cold in Canada. Toronto's not too bad, but the *rest* of Canada!" I hear him laugh on the other side of the phone. Of course, he's not taking me seriously. Why would he? I'm making a complete fool of myself.

"Anyway, all that to say that I find you very attractive, and if I were some kind of Victoria's Secret model like your girlfriend, I would want you to come over right now. But I'm not. A Victoria's Secret model, or your girlfriend for that matter. So instead, I thought I would call you and tell you this, and probably add this to the extensive list of embarrassing things I've done in my life. Although, let's be honest this takes the crown spot. Yes. So. On that note. It was nice having met you last night. Again, thank you for helping me with Stuart. I owe you one. Oh and do you like being called Mav? I was just wondering. Also, my roommate, Catherine, she works at Weis Books, a tiny publishing company here in Toronto. Her name's Catherine Deck. Please take a look into her and her work. Okay. So. Thank you. Goodbye."

I quickly press the red button on my screen and place my phone on the wooden coffee table. I sit in silence for a moment, realizing what I had just done. I slowly reach over the couch and grab one of the cushions I had bought last year. Light grey, with dark green swirls. I bring the cushion up my face and scream into it. A long scream, just enough to get some of my frustrations out. How could I be so stupid and do something that foolish?

I pick up my glass of wine and take a small sip. I grab my book from the coffee table and flip it open, picking up where I left off not long ago, letting myself become submersed in a fantasy world, instead of my own.

CHAPTER FOUR

There's a knock on the door. I'm deep in my book and jump at the sound of knuckles on wood. I place my book down on the coffee table and stand up, adjusting my red plaid pajama pants. I didn't expect Catherine to be home until later. Even when she has an awful date, she sticks it out to the end of dinner.

I swing open the door half expecting to see Catherine, but instead, it's Maverick. He's standing in the hall, a bouquet of multicoloured roses in one hand. A small heart shaped box of chocolates and a small, pink, plush toy monkey in the other.

"Happy Valentine's Day." He smiles at me. My jaw drops at the sight of him. Not for a moment did I think my calling him would result in him showing up at my front door. I can't help but watch him. All of him. From his shiny dress shoes and navy-blue suit to his hair, styled neatly to one side. I briefly wonder just how many dark blue suits he owns.

I try to speak but no words come out. I slowly shake my head, in shock at what I was seeing.

"You came." I finally say. Softly. My voice just above a whisper. My hand slowly comes up to my face, covering my mouth. The other arm wrapping around my torso. Maverick takes a step closer to me. "You called." His smile disappears and his eyes briefly drop to my lips before finding my eyes again. His voice serious. "I'm glad you called, Jessica."

"You are?"

"I was hoping to see you before I left."

I sharply inhale, and the horrifying realization hits me. I'm wearing pajamas.

"Oh my god."

Maverick frowns, "Is everything alright?"

"No. I mean, it will be." I move from the door, making space for him to come in. Maverick walks past me. I can smell his cologne waft behind him. It smelled warm and mysterious, inviting. It left me wanting to breathe it all in. I close the door behind us, and he turns around to face me once more. He comes closer to me, closing the gap between us.

"I thought I would get you a little something for Valentine's Day." He speaks quietly, never breaking eye contact.

I take the box of chocolates and the toy monkey from him, smiling.

"Do you have a vase I can put these in?" he asks, his voice low.

"Cabinet above the fridge." I say, meeting his gaze.

"I am going to go change into something a bit more appropriate." I chuckle looking down at my pajama pants and tattered Guardians of the Galaxy t-shirt.

"I think you look cute." He says looking down at my ensemble of an outfit. I smile and turn on my heel heading to my bedroom.

"I want to take you out to dinner. Dress accordingly." He calls behind me. I nod back at him and hurry off to my bedroom, clenching the soft monkey to my chest.

When I enter the living room, Maverick is sitting on the blue couch flipping through the pages of my book. He turns his head as I walk across the living room. I can see his chest expand as he inhales seeing me. He smiles and shakes his head, lowering his gaze to the floor before looking back up at me.

"You are so beautiful." He exhales, looking deep into my eyes. I feel my cheeks are red and hot and I look over my shoulder trying not to blush any harder, finding the small painting of a cow in a field to look at while my face goes back to its normal tone. He stands from the couch and slides his hands in his pockets. He begins to walk over toward me.

"Threads of Power. Nice reading choice." He nods approvingly.

I can't help but smile. I fiddle with my fingers as he comes closer. He takes slow steps, but the apartment is so small that he's in front of me within a couple steps. He's close enough that I can feel his breath when he speaks.

"Michael is downstairs." He says sort of matter-of-factly. I inhale loudly, watching his lips move as he speaks.

"We shouldn't keep him waiting." I whisper, unable to stop staring at his mouth. Maverick brings his hand up to my face and moves a stray hair behind my ear.

"Usually, I don't go by Mav." He frowns, "But want *you* to call me Mav."

I look into his eyes, getting lost in the dark green colour. I nod.

He puts his hand on the small of my back and leads me out the front door, grabbing our coats on the way out.

We approach the familiar jet-black Cadillac and Michael is standing by the back door. He smiles when he sees me.

"Good evening, Jessica." He opens the door as we walk up the vehicle.

"Hi, Michael." I give him a small wave as I climb into the car. Michael closes the door, and the two men walk over to the opposite side of the car, climbing in. The car's engine purrs to life, and we begin down the road. The Cadillac looks out of place in the small, poor neighbourhood. Dressed the way we are, the three of us also look out of place.

I watch the cars driving along the road and ask Mav, "So, where are we going?"

"What fun would it be if I told you and ruined the surprise?"

I look over at him. He has a boyish grin across his face. I laugh and lean back into the smooth leather seat.

We drive for a half hour – the joys of living in the city – before we arrive at the Ritz-Carlton. The car stops in front of the revolving glass doors. Maverick exits the car first, waving away the valet who was making his way to the car.

"Enjoy your evening" Michael smiles at me through the rear-view mirror.

"Thanks. Have a good evening." I smile sweetly at Michael.

Maverick opens my door and helps me out of the tall car. As he closes the door behind me, Michael drives away.

I wonder where he goes when Mav doesn't need him.

I look over at Maverick as he offers his elbow. He's towering over me. I weave my arm through his elbow and rest my hand on his forearm. The wind is spinning around us, the cold biting its way through my coat. We walk into the expensive hotel lobby together. We walk to the Restaurant at the far end of the hotel lobby. At the entrance there's a sharply dressed waiter that greets us.

"Reservation for Maverick Walker." Mav instructs the young waiter as we approach.

The waiter smiles at us, his bright blonde hair neatly combed backwards. "You may follow me, Mr. and Mrs. Walker." And he sets off at a quick pace toward the end of the restaurant. We follow. I open my mouth to comment on the 'Mrs. Walker' comment but quickly decide to just let it slide since it didn't seem to bother Maverick. We walk through the dimly lit restaurant. Low hanging lights above the tables, and greenery across the walls. As we walk, I can hear the low chatter of people having dinner, and in the background, soft jazz music.

The waiter opens a door at the back wall, and enters, gesturing for us to follow. Maverick and I enter the small, open room. There is a table in the centre with a placemat, utensils, and a tall candle in the centre. The room is dimly lit. Beautiful paintings lined the walls.

The young waiter leaves a few menus on the table for us.

"I'll be back shortly." He smiles and exits the room, closing the door behind him.

I let go of Mavericks arm and he comes around behind me, removing my coat and hanging it on the back of my chair. He pulls out the chair for me, and I politely sit. As he tucks in the chair, I look up at him and murmur "Thanks." He smiles in response and makes his way to the opposite side of the table.

"Wow, this is beautiful." My eyes dance around the room as Maverick removes his own coat and sits in his chair, facing me. While I take in the beauty of the room, Maverick sits across from me, staring. Not at the walls or the room, but at me. After a bit, I can't help but look at him. He is beyond gorgeous. His brown hair neatly combed over, with one wavy strand falling over his forehead. He was resting his chin in his hand, his index finger covering the middle of his mouth.

I pick up the menu and begin flipping through the pages. The waiter enters with a bottle of champagne.

"The bottle you ordered earlier, Mr. Walker." He presents the bottle to Maverick.

Maverick gives the waiter a small nod as he opens the bottle and begins to pour two glasses.

I whisper, "Thank you." As the waiter slides my glass to me and leaves the room.

I look up at Maverick. He raises his glass, "To this fine evening, with the most beautiful girl I've ever had the pleasure of meeting." We clink our glasses, and take a sip, never breaking eye contact.

"So," I start, my confidence suddenly raising. "How did you manage to get all this?"

"Easy. I saw you yesterday. Made a reservation and waited for your call."

"Hmm."

"I normally get what I want. This time I just wanted to make sure you wanted it too."

"Okay, tell me this then: Why me?"

Maverick smiles and looks down at the table before looking deep into my eyes. Sitting extremely still with an intense look in his eye.

"I find you very mysterious, Jessica. You're beautiful, you have character, and there is so much about you I want to know."

I blush. Hard. My cheeks are probably the same colour of the red dress I took out of Catherine's closet.

"Now, I would ask you the same question, but you emptied your heart out over the phone." He chuckles, his smile inviting. "That was brave. Most people would not have been able to do that."

"Sorry about that." I raise my eyebrows.

"Don't you dare apologize for that! Tell me, do you regret being here right now?"

"No."

"Then you shouldn't be apologizing. Your call made this possible."

"Speaking of the call, my roommate, Catherine..."

Maverick waves his hand, and frowns.

"I'm on a date with *you,* not Catherine. If it calms you down though, I sent her information to my assistant. She's going to take care of it."

I smile up at Maverick and the waiter walks into the room.

We get up from the table and I grab my coat from the back of the chair. Maverick glides towards me. He stands just behind my shoulder, his head lowered to my ear. I could once again smell the warmth of his cologne.

"Could I interest you in a cup of coffee upstairs?" His voice is low, and gruff.

I look to my shoulder, seeing Maverick in my peripheral vision. I quietly inhale the mysterious cologne, and nod slowly.

"I would like that." My voice quiet and slow. He gently puts his hands on my hip bone and leads me out of the restaurant. My heart is pounding in my throat, and I swallow hard. His hand feels warm, and safe. Strong, but he holds it gently on my hip.

We approach the elevators and Maverick presses the button without letting go of me. He turns to face me, his hand still resting on my hip. His free hand reaches up and strokes my cheek with his thumb. I close my eyes and lean my face into his hand. His hand is soft. His thumb slides down my cheek and under my chin. I open my eyes and gently, he lifts my chin toward his face.

"I've been thinking about you all day. I can't keep it in, it's driving me crazy. I can't stop thinking about you." He's frowning, his gaze going from one eye to the other.

The elevator doors open with a *ding*. He drops his hand from my chin, and we enter the elevator. Behind us, an older couple hurry to enter. I smile at the lady who goes to stand beside me. Maverick's hand tightens around my waist, and he brings me closer to him. The older man hits the button for the 5th floor and looks to us.

"Penthouse, please." Maverick says.

My eyes widen and I look up at Maverick, shocked. He doesn't meet my gaze. Instead, he stares forward, smiling proudly to himself.

The elevator ascends smoothly and the four of us ride in silence. The older couple exchanging glances with each other, clearly both thinking about Maverick and his penthouse.

The elevator stops at the 5th floor and the doors slide open.

"Have a nice evening." The lady smiles at us as her husband's grabs her hand and leads her out of the elevator.

I smile shyly and wave to her. As the doors close, I shoot a look at Maverick.

"You didn't tell me you own the penthouse!"

"There are lots of things I haven't told you yet." He looks down at me.

"But all in due time. I want to take my time with you, Jess."

My stomach turns. There's a warm, longing sensation between my legs. I break the eye contact and look around the elevator, taking in its sleek look. Mirrors all along the top half of the elevator walls. The bottom half, a warm beige panel. With a *ding* the elevator arrives at the top and we exit into a small hallway. At the end of the hall is a large wooden door with potted plants on either side. The walls are light beige with a hint of grey. There are large paintings lining the walls, with thick white trims running around the door, floor, and ceiling.

    Maverick approaches the door and slides a key into the keyhole. With a low *click* he opens the door and gestures for me to enter. I walk in and notice that all his penthouse is in shades of grey and silver. He follows me, closing the door behind us. I hang my coat on a silver coat rack beside the door. Maverick throws his onto a small grey ottoman in the foyer and makes his way to the kitchen.

    "What kind of coffee would you like?" He calls from the kitchen. "I can make just about anything with this new machine."

    "An iced coffee, please. If you can." I say wandering around the living room, taking in the sights of his penthouse. Large glass windows showed the CN Tower and the lake below. The CN Tower illuminated in red. I sit down on the long grey couch across from the fireplace stood in the center of the room. I notice a large book on the coffee table. It has a large Canvas cover, with red sprayed edges and in red text '*WONDERLAND Annie Leibovitz*'. I flip through the pages admiring the photographs. After a few minutes, Maverick walks out of the kitchen, a tall glass in one hand a plain grey mug in the other. How obsessed with grey is he? Even his mugs are grey.

He sets the two down on the coffee table and sits beside me. Close enough that our knees almost touch.

"I see you're a fan of photography." I say picking up my glass.

"It's a passion." He points to the large prints on his walls, "I took all those photographs."

His walls had canvases all over with photographs printed onto them. Most of them cityscapes and street photography. All of them black and white – surprise, surprise.

"Hmm." I drink my coffee, "You're a CEO, you're handsome, you're rich, you're talented. Is there anything you can't do, Maverick Walker?"

Maverick audibly inhales and bites his bottom lip. He looks at me, his mind running.

"There is one thing. But you cannot tell anyone. Ever."

"Oooh. My ninth graders are gonna love this."

He laughs loudly.

"Now you need to promise me you won't tell anyone. Even your ninth graders. Even though I doubt they even know who I am."

"Mmm. I can't promise you anything. It all depends what your secret it." I say cheekily, looking Maverick up and down.

"You're lucky you're cute, Jess." He shakes his head. I feel my face go red.

"Okay, the truth is, I can't swim."

I almost choke on my coffee.

"You can't swim? You can build a successful publishing company, but you can't swim?"

Maverick shrugs. "I didn't learn as a kid, and by the time I became an adult I figured it would be easier to avoid swimming than it would be to learn."

I begin to laugh, of all the things in the world, swimming is not what I imagined Maverick Walker being unable to do. I continue laughing, Maverick is watching. His face calm, but his eyes quickly go fierce.

I finish laughing and he slides himself closer, his body turns facing me. He gets close enough that I can feel his breath on my skin.

"Kiss me."

I stare into his eyes. They're fierce. There's hunger in them. I want him.

"Kiss me, Jessica. Kiss me and I can become your first love."

My eyes drop down to his lips. He wets them and I feel like kissing him would fix all the problems in the world. Like he has the ability to make everything right with one kiss. One magnificent kiss.

He sits silently, staring deep into my eyes. So deep that I could get lost in his dark green eyes forever. Lost in the beautiful colours.

I lunge toward Maverick and our lips lock. He reaches his hands up and cups my face, his hands warm, gentle. I rest my hand onto his thigh. I can feel his body tense under my touch, and he inhales. He kisses me harder, parting my lips with his. He reaches one hand to the back of my neck, tousling my hair. I feel his tongue reach into my mouth as he explores the tips of my teeth. He pulls me closer to him, bringing my leg onto his. He moves his mouth away from mine and brushes his lips against my jaw and leaves a trail of kisses down my neck.

I fight back a moan. I arch my neck backwards, pushing into his lips. I feel him smile against my neck. He brushes his long fingers down my arm, across my waist, and rests his hand on my thigh. I shiver, even though the apartment isn't cold. Maverick brings his mouth next to my ear. He squeezes my thigh, and I let out a whimper.

He chuckles quietly and growls my name into my ear. I push my legs together, feeling a pool forming in my underwear. I run my hand up Maverick's arm, feeling his muscles tense against his tight shirt.

"Oh, Jessica." He growls, "Oh, how I've been waiting for this moment. How I've been waiting for you."

He wants me. He really wants me.

Maverick gently bites the lobe of my ear and tugs on it before letting go. I expect to feel pain, but instead I get a feeling deep in my belly, wanting him. I inhale sharply and turn my head to face Maverick. His eyes dark and ferocious. I stare at his lips. A smile widens across his face, and I lean in to kiss him. His lips wet, warm.

"Maverick," I breathe into his mouth, 'Mav."

"Yes, darling." He responds, his breath jagged trying to kiss me enough before the night is over, before he needs to go back home.

I pull back and watch him, watch him trying to catch his breath. A cheeky smile appears across my lips before I turn on my knee and straddle him. Kissing him harder, listening to Maverick moan against my mouth.

His hands tighten around my waist.

"Fuck." He whispers against my mouth and reaches down to adjust himself. He runs his hand up my thigh and it disappears under my red dress where it cuts down the side of the leg, just below the hip. I feel his thumb brushing the lacy band of my underwear. My hips tense as he runs his thumb along the hem towards my belly. He gently runs his middle finger down the centre of my underwear. Instinctively I tilt my pelvis towards his touch. He kisses the side of my neck, nibbling gently as he strokes the thin layer of fabric between them.

My breathing is ragged as I clutch the back of Maverick's neck, ruffling his hair in my hands. I feel him smile against my neck as he moves my underwear aside and slides his finger into me. I moan into his wavy, and now messy, hair as though something inside me had just broken. My knees begin to feel wobbly.

His finger still inside me, Maverick gently twists my body off him and lays me down across the couch.

"Mmm, you want it bad, don't you?" He growls into my neck, his finger curling. I whimper, nodding. My fingers tighten around his neck.

"All in due time, Jessica." And he slowly withdraws his hand and I'm left wanting more. I open my eyes seeing Maverick, sitting up, his handsome face looking down at me, thinking about all the things he wants to do with me. To me.

He unbuttons his white shirt and throws it off to the side of the living room. My eyes wandering across his chiseled chest, down his abs, and falling towards the bulge in his pants. I push my legs together imagining what he must feel like. He leans over me, his hair falling overtop his face. He grabs the sides of my dress and slides it off me. He throws it to the side, inhaling as he takes in the sight of me.

I let my leg slide off the side of the couch, silently inviting him back. He throws himself at me, kissing me harder than he's ever kissed me. He strokes my hair with his hand and inhales the smell of my perfume. He slides his hand across my back, searching for my bra clasp. With one swift motion he undoes it and returns his hand to my front to remove my bra and throw it with the rest of our clothes.

"Jessica, I've wanted you since I first saw you." He whispers to me, and makes his way down to my chest, kissing me as he goes. He cups one breast with his hand, squeezing, kneading. His mouth finds its way to my other breast, his tongue flicking the nipple as he continues lower. My breath shudders as he reaches down to my underwear. Looking up at me, he begins to peel the underwear away from me. I become suddenly aware of the grey nylon couch underneath me. He drops the underwear to the floor and his mouth continues where he had left off.

He kisses around my belly button and brushes his smooth lips down to my inner thigh. His middle finger had sneaked its way between my legs and with one swift motion disappeared between my legs once more. I exhale, curling my hips towards Maverick. He kisses my inner thighs, until I feel his tongue against me, sucking the most sensitive part of me, his finger stroking me. I writhe under his touch. My body on fire as his face works between my legs. His mouth and finger working in complete unison, my heart pounds against my ribs, experiencing something I never have before.

"Mav." I whisper between breaths.

He growls against me.

"Mav, I'm gonna come." I manage to choke out just before it happens, and I give in to the pleasure. Maverick's grip tightens on me, and he groans, approving of what he had done. My legs are shaking, my body is shaking. I pull his head away just as I lean back against the couch, closing my eyes, catching my breath.

When I open my eyes again, Maverick is lying next to me on the couch, smiling to himself. Satisfied.

I roll onto my side, wanting more of Maverick. I can feel the warmth of the fireplace on my skin. I keep my eyes on him as I reach down and begin undoing his belt and sliding his pants down. He swallows hard but doesn't break eye contact. I slide his pants off and run my fingers up his legs. He inhales, watching me. I reach the hem of his boxers and slow my fingers, gently brushing them up his balls, reaching his cock. He moans, his hips tensing. Under my hand, I feel him throbbing. I look down, seeing his massive package, the tip sticking out just above the band of his boxers.

My voice shudders.

"I need you, Mav." He inhales sharply. "I need you now, I needed you yesterday."

I slide his boxers off, freeing him, and throw them towards the kitchen. Wasting no time, I get on top of him, straddling him.

CHAPTER FIVE

I wake up Sunday morning in bed alone. In Maverick's bed. I look around the room searching for my clothes. They're nowhere to be seen.

Probably still downstairs.

I get out of bed, admiring the city in the bright winter morning light. I walk over to Maverick's dresser and find an oversized black t-shirt along with a pair of dark grey boxers. I slide them on and make my way out to the kitchen.

The apartment is warm, and comfortable. I walk into the kitchen and Maverick is standing at the island counter, cutting fruits. He's shirtless, wearing only a pair of long, blue pajama pants. His biceps tense as he cuts up an apple. He looks up as I enter the kitchen, smiling at me.

"Good morning, beautiful." His smile widens, and I can see bright white teeth. "I like the look." He points at the shirt.

I sit down on a stool opposite to him.

"I hope you don't mind," I start, "I guess I left my clothes in the living room."

"I already put them in the laundry." He slides a hot cup of coffee toward me. The rich smell of coffee beans, filling my nose.

I notice my phone that I had left the evening prior and reach over, grabbing it while Maverick went back to cutting fruits.

I turn it on and find a bunch of missed messages from Catherine.

JESSICA.

HOLY SHIT I'M PROUD OF YOU.

I GOT HOME EARLY THIS MORNING AND I WAS SURPRISED TO FIND THAT YOU WERE NOT HERE.

I NEVER EXPECTED THIS.

YOU ARE GOING TO NEED TO TELL ME ALL ABOUT IT WHEN YOU GET HOME.

WAS HE GOOD?

WHAT DID YOU SAY TO HIM?

AH I CANNOT WAIT FOR YOU TO COME HOME

I mean, take your time. I just want to know what happened.

Okay.

See you whenever.

I smile at phone.

"Catherine?" Maverick asks assembling a plate with fruits, and some waffles.

"Yeah," I nod "She's home and noticed that I wasn't, so she was just wondering where I was."

"Something tells me she knows exactly where you are." He slides a plate with breakfast, and a fork to me as I blush.

"Maybe something about her being 'scary'." He says raising an eyebrow. I chuckle.

"It's not that she's *scary...*"

"Jess, you don't need to explain,"

"She's just an overprotective best friend."

Maverick watches me, smiling, his hands leaning on the counter.

"So, it's not that she's scary, that should be no reason that you don't hire her."

"My assistant is going to call Catherine this week, offering her a job."

"What?"

"You heard me. My assistant sent me an email this morning saying she loved the work Catherine does. So, I decided that I will hire her to work at my Toronto office."

I almost cry. Catherine is going to freak out. I grab the fork and begin eating, my head swirling with thoughts of Maverick, Catherine, and again, Maverick. We eat breakfast in silence, and I am oblivious to the fact that I'm slowly falling in love with Maverick Walker.

"Thank you, Mav." I say forking a piece of melon and bringing it to my mouth.

Mav smiles, watching me as he takes a sip from his coffee cup.

He frowns and places the cup to the side of his plate.

"Listen," he starts.

Oh crap. This can't be good.

I place my fork down and prepare for the worst.

"As you know, I live in Montreal." He continues.

"Yeah, you've told me."

"But I don't want to throw away what we've started."

I tilt my head. That is the opposite of what I thought he would say. I look down at the lonely waffle laying in my plate, my head spinning.

"I'll need to leave to catch my flight soon, how about I call you this week and we discuss it?"

I nod, sipping my hot coffee, but a feeling deep in my gut tells me this is the last I'll see of Maverick. I fight back tears and start eating the waffle.

THE ONE NIGHT VALENTINE

We eat our breakfast in silence. I never even look up at Mav. He begins to clean the counter and I excuse myself to the bathroom, where I grab my clothes and change. The bathroom is brightly lit, and impeccably clean. As if no one has ever used it.

I rinse my face with cold water and lean overtop the sink, taking deep, steadying breaths.

What have I gotten myself into?

I straighten and look in the mirror. I could barely recognise myself. I seem... happy. Even though I'm scared I may never see Maverick again. I wipe my hands on the white towel hanging on the wall opposite the sink, pushing away the thoughts clouding my mind.

I take a deep breath before exiting the bathroom.

When I enter the living room, Maverick is sitting on the couch, typing something on his laptop.

I stop a few meters from the back of the couch.

"Umm, I probably should get home. I have some grading I need to finish for my classes tomorrow." I say, unable to look him in the eye.

Maverick shuts his laptop and looks at me.

"Okay." He says, "Can I drive you home?"

I smile, and nod. Maverick smiles back and stands up. We make our way to his spacious foyer. Maverick takes my coat off the hanger, his eyebrows furrowing as he looks at it.

"Surely this thing can't be warm." He says helping me put my coat on.

"It's really not." I admit, chuckling.

"Hmm."

I turn to face him as he begins putting on his coat. I watch the coat come flush against his muscled back. My mind quickly wandering back to the events of last night. I blush and try to shake the memory out of my mind – at least for the time being.

He extends his hand toward me. I reach out and he closes his hand on mine, leading me out of the penthouse apartment. His hand is warm around mine, and for a moment I feel like we're an actual couple.

We walk up to the black Cadillac outside. Michael walks over to the passenger door and helps me in. Snow swirling around us. The door closes and I watch Maverick say something to Michael. Michael nods and begins walking to the hotel doors. Maverick walks around the car and climbs in the driver's seat.

"I didn't know you drive." I say looking at him.

He laughs and turns the key in the ignition. I watch his fingers flex around the steering wheel as he begins to drive away from the hotel.

We spend the rest of the drive in silence. I lazily look out the window, watching cars, pedestrians. My mind in deep thoughts of Maverick, and our situationship. Can I just let go of what happened between us? Can I just go back to my boring day-to-day life? Can I forget about him and move on?

Maverick parks the car on the street in front of my apartment building. He takes the key out of the ignition and begins climbing out of the car. I open the car door and hop out of the car. He frowns as he walks up to me.

"I was going to open the door for you." He says closing the space between us.

"I can open my own door. I can do things on my own." I retort.

He exhales, his throat bobbing. "But you don't always have to." He calmly responds.

I bite my cheek. The snow falling harder around us. I wipe some snowflakes off Maverick's shoulder. I feel him tense under my hand. I run my hand down his arm, feeling his biceps under my touch. He's silent. Watching me as I slide my hand into his.

Intertwining our fingers and leading him towards the building where the cold couldn't get us.

    I take my keys out of my pocket and tap the black, oval key fob to the door lock and the door buzzes, unlocking. Maverick opens the glass door and follows me into the building. We cross the lobby towards the elevator. There are a few teenagers sitting on the old beige couches to the left, chatting amongst themselves. As we walk by them, two of the girls stare at Maverick. Their jaws dropping. They quickly turn their gaze away, still trying to take sneaky glances at him. Their faces bright red. The three boys sitting with them, oblivious to our existence. I push the button for the elevator and turn to face Maverick. I notice the girls giggling to each other. Quickly I remember what it was like being 15 years old, living in Toronto, and seeing handsome men in suits making their way to work. Talking with my girlfriends, imagining what it would be like in ten years, when we're older and have super-hot boyfriends. I realize that I am living the moment that 15-year-old Jess dreamed of. That I am living the moment that those two teenage girls imagine of.

    "You alright?" Maverick asks, hooking his index finger under my chin and bringing my gaze to him.

    I stare into his green eyes. I can't let him go back to Montreal without telling him how I feel.

"No," I start. His brow furrows and he frowns looking into my eyes.

"But it will be." I continue, "I'm going to make sure of it."

Maverick wraps his hands around my waist and pulls me closer to him.

"I like the idea of you taking charge. Jessica." Maverick's gaze darkens and a wicked smile appears. He kisses my forehead, and the elevator door opens behind me. I pull away from Maverick and head into the elevator, looking over my shoulder at him. He digs his hands into his pockets and follows me, his smile cheeky, his gaze looking at my butt. I click the button for the 7th floor and lean my back against the mirrored wall of the elevator. The light bulb flickering – as always. Maverick stands beside me leaning against the wall as well. Hands still in his pockets. He looks down at his shoes. The door closes slowly. A bit too slowly. The elevator jolts to action.

Maverick shuts his eyes and grunts. Deep in his throat. In one swift motion, Mavericks turns toward me, bringing me against his muscular body, one hand going through my hair, and his tongue parting my lips. He catches me off guard and I stumble backwards, his large hands pressing me closer to him, keeping me from falling entirely. I lean into his touch and run my hand up his back. My other hand gripping onto his bicep. Our lips locked, and I forget where we are. I feel Maverick's warmth, strength, encompassing me. He maneuvers his tongue through my mouth with skilled ease. His fingers wrap around my hair, gently tugging, my mouth opening slightly wider for him.

Maverick grunts into my mouth. Our bodies are pressed against each other that I can feel him growing bigger.

For a couple floors, Maverick and I are intertwined, our lips locked. The elevator shutters to a stop and the door begins to slowly open. Maverick turns back around and leans against the wall once more. The door opens and a woman is standing with her young son. Her eyes widen as she brings her son closer to her and ushers him into the corner of the elevator. I bring my hand up to my mouth, trying to hide the stupid grin I can't get rid of. Maverick nods his head to the woman as she passes by and says, "Nice day, isn't it?"

As the elevator rattles to life again, Maverick clears his throat and smiles into the distance.

It isn't long before the elevator once again shakily rolls to a stop. As the door slides open, Maverick hooks his hand around my waist, and we exit the elevator. As we leave, I see the woman relax her grip on the young boy. We walk in silence toward my apartment. A few meters before the door I suddenly stop and turn to face Maverick.

Like a band-aid, Jess.

"Mav, I need to tell you something," I start.

Maverick watches me, his eyes intense, listening to every word I'm saying.

"What we have going on, is good. I don't think we can just throw that away." My voice cracks and tears start welling inside my eyes. Maverick takes a step closer, resting his hands on my upper arms.

"There's nothing that I wouldn't do to keep you in my life, Jess. I'm not saying you should move to Montreal right this week or anything, but I can't let you go. I don't want to lose you. Ever. I want to be the one you come to when you've had a bad day, a good day. I want to be the person that makes you love life. I want to make memories with you. I want to be the most important man in your life. Give me a chance, and I will make you feel like you could touch the edge of heaven."

My eyes burn with the tears that I'm fighting back. One of them escapes and I quickly wipe it off with my palm. The smile I had in the elevator quickly returning.

Maverick leans a bit looking at the wet spot on my cheek where my tear had rolled.

"Is that a happy tear?" He asks cautiously. I laugh, nodding my head vigorously. The tears now rolling down my face. I fling myself at Maverick. Wrapping my arms around his neck. He smiles audibly. Wrapping his strong arms around my torso. Nuzzling his face into my neck.

I let go of him and grab his hand. My free hand reaching up to wipe the tears off my face.

"Do you want to come in for a cup of coffee?" I ask, steadying my breath.

"How could I say no?" Maverick responds, keeping his eyes on me as we walk to my apartment door. Our steps silent on the musty carpet underneath.

"I can't let you live here though." He says.

"It's fine." I laugh.

"I don't think this carpet has ever been washed. Carpet shouldn't smell like this."

"Oh, so you're an expert in carpets now?"

"No, but I do know that my girlfriend and her roommate, who just so happens to be working for me, deserve to live somewhere respectable."

"Because smelly carpets, and rackety old elevators aren't respectable?"

"No. End of discussion." Maverick is smiling at me. I laugh, squeezing his hand, as we walk up to my apartment door.

EPILOGUE

THREE MONTHS LATER

I walk down the streets of Montreal, checking the time on my watch as I approach a tall, glass-covered building. There's still ten minutes before Maverick leaves for lunch. We were supposed to meet at a local café for lunch, but I decided to surprise him at his office instead. I enter the building. The lobby is empty, clean, grey. I walk towards the silver elevator doors, walking past the two ladies at the front desk. One of them smiles at me, the other waves calling in a cheery voice, "Good morning, Ms. Aydin."

I wave at them both and continue to the elevator. The doors slide open, and I enter. The interior is covered on all sides with mirrors. Floor to ceiling. I click the button for the top floor checking my watch again. My heart is pounding against my ribcage as I tighten the belt of my long black trench coat, a gift from Maverick. The elevator stops with a *ding* and the doors slide open. I walk out into the sharply furnished room. A small waiting area with grey seats and a low coffee table, also grey. In large letter on the wall *WALKER PUBLICATIONS*. I walk toward the tall silver desk just next to a set of large dark grey double doors. The young man at the desk smiles at me.

"Ms. Aydin, what a nice surprise! Mr. Walker was just getting ready to come see you. You can go on in." He smiles getting up from his desk and opening one of the doors for me.

"Thanks, James." I smile at him, entering the large office of my now boyfriend, Maverick Walker.

He's standing overtop his desk looking through a stack of papers. He looks up and his eyes light up when he sees me standing by the door.

"Jessica. I'm surprised to see you here." He says calmly, straightening his back.

I remove my coat and hang it on the coat rack off to the side. His office is spacious, and clean. Everything in shades of grey and silver, of course. Seriously, what is it with this man and grey? I walk over and hug him tight, feeling the warmth of his body against mine. March in Quebec was still horribly cold, and I was happy to be warming up in his office. I let go of him and walk across to his desk. He sits on the edge of the desk, crossing his arms.

"So, what brings you here?" He asks.

I look out the windows of his office, looking over the city, the river. In the distance, La Ronde. I bite my bottom lip. My smile cheeky like the Cheshire cats. Without breaking eye contact I reach down and undo my belt, letting my long coat fall to the floor.

Maverick's eyes widen, his gaze drops, as I'm standing in front of him in my nicest lingerie set.

"Are you hungry, Mav?"

Piper S. Grey

COMING SOON

WELCOME TO GRAEME PLACE

What do you do when your little brother goes missing in a town known for children's kidnappings?

When Addie-May Miller moves to a small town in Ontario with her family, she suggests a game of hide-and-seek to her little brother, Lucas. Lucas finds an overhead door in one of the closets that leads him to the attic.

An investigation begins on the property and surrounding areas, with search-and-rescue teams working days on end. Upon further research, Addie-May discovers that this isn't the first time a child goes missing in that house. With that in mind, Addie-May takes it upon herself to find her brother.

Welcome to Graeme Place is a story of bravery, and sibling love. Filled with ghosts, and evil kings. How far are you willing to go to save the one you love? Or someone you may not even know at all?

OTHER BOOKS BY THE AUTHOR

HAVE A HOLLY JOLLY SNOWMAGEDDON

For Andi, the holidays are an opportunity to work overtime, distracting her from the holiday season. This year, the weather takes a turn for the worst and the staff and guests of the Whispering Pines Inn get trapped by a large snowstorm taking over the province. Ben, a handsome, brown-haired co-worker gets trapped with Andi. Together, they work to keep the inn's guests safe and warm and discover romantic feelings for one another.

ABOUT THE AUTHOR

Hi! I'm Piper!

I am an Indie author, and freelance professional photographer. I live with my boyfriend, and orange cat, Watson, in the beautiful Canadian province, Quebec.

I love incorporating different Canadian locations in my work, showing readers the beauty of Canada's landscapes one page at a time (And reminding people that Canada is in fact a country, and no we don't say "aboot" – We do however eat maple syrup off snow...).

I am a huge mental health advocate, and strive to use my stories as a means of educating others, and helping people feel less lonely in their thoughts, situations, emotions, etc.